Winter Hunting

Living in a Shoe

SHEEP

How to build a BRIDGE

WORKOUT TAPE

FOX

BIG Fa

Jack Nimble

E
Oma

O'Malley, Kevin

Humpty Dumpty
egg-splodes

DUE DATE	BRODART	08/01	16.85

"'It followed her to school one day, which was against the rules.'

Does anybody know what happens next?

Anybody?
No?

Well, she found a giant egg crushing the school. It wasn't just any egg, oh no. It was an . . .

EGG-CEEDINGLY Large HUMPTY DUMPTY."

For Emily,
my editor

First published in the United States of America in 2001 by Walker Publishing Company, Inc.
Published simultaneously in Canada by Fitzhenry and Whiteside, Markham, Ontario L3R 4T8

Library of Congress Cataloging-in-Publication Data

O'Malley, Kevin, 1961–
    Humpty Dumpty egg-splodes / Kevin O'Malley.
        p.   cm.
    Summary: An enormous Humpty Dumpty returns to seek revenge on the
    nursery rhyme characters who let him fall.
    ISBN 0-8027-8756-8 (hc) — ISBN 0-8027-8757-6 (rein)
    [1. Nursery rhymes—Fiction. 2. Characters in literature—Fiction.] I. Title.
    PZ7.O526 Hu 2001
    [FIC]—dc21
                                                        00-043777

Book design by Sophie Ye Chin

Printed in Hong Kong
10 9 8 7 6 5 4 3 2 1

"Humpty Dumpty," said Mary, "what happened to you? You're huge!"

"That's right, I'm huge, and I'm not gonna take it anymore."

"What are you talking about?" asked Mary.

"Oh, you know darn well. 'Oh look, the tubby bald eggman is falling off the wall, haa, haa, haa.' Did anybody ever think how painful it would be to have a horse try to put you back together?

No.

So I'm back, baby."

Say good-bye to Mother Goose Land!

Old King Cole was a merry old soul until Jack came running in.
"What? Humpty Dumpty's gonna wreck the town?" exclaimed the king.
"What am I supposed to do? I'm not a smart king, just a merry one.
The real brains of the town is Mother Goose,
and she's away on vacation getting her feathers fluffed."

"Well, you'd better think of something quick," said Jack.
"Humpty Dumpty's headed this way!"

"I've got it," said Old King Cole. "Get me Peter Piper."

"Peter Piper," said the king. "Pick me a peck of pickled peppers.
Then throw them at Humpty Dumpty.
He hates pickled peppers."

"Your Highness, it didn't work. Humpty just ate the peppers," reported Jack.

"How many pecks of pickled peppers
did Peter Piper pick?" asked the king.

"He pitched pickled peppers until he was positively pooped.
Should I try calling Mother Hubbard?" asked Jack.

"Naw, what's she got to throw at Humpty?
Her cupboard is always bare.
Besides, she's never at home and you'd end up talking to that smart aleck dog.
Let's call the grand old Duke of York," said the king.

Good idea!
He's got ten
thousand men.

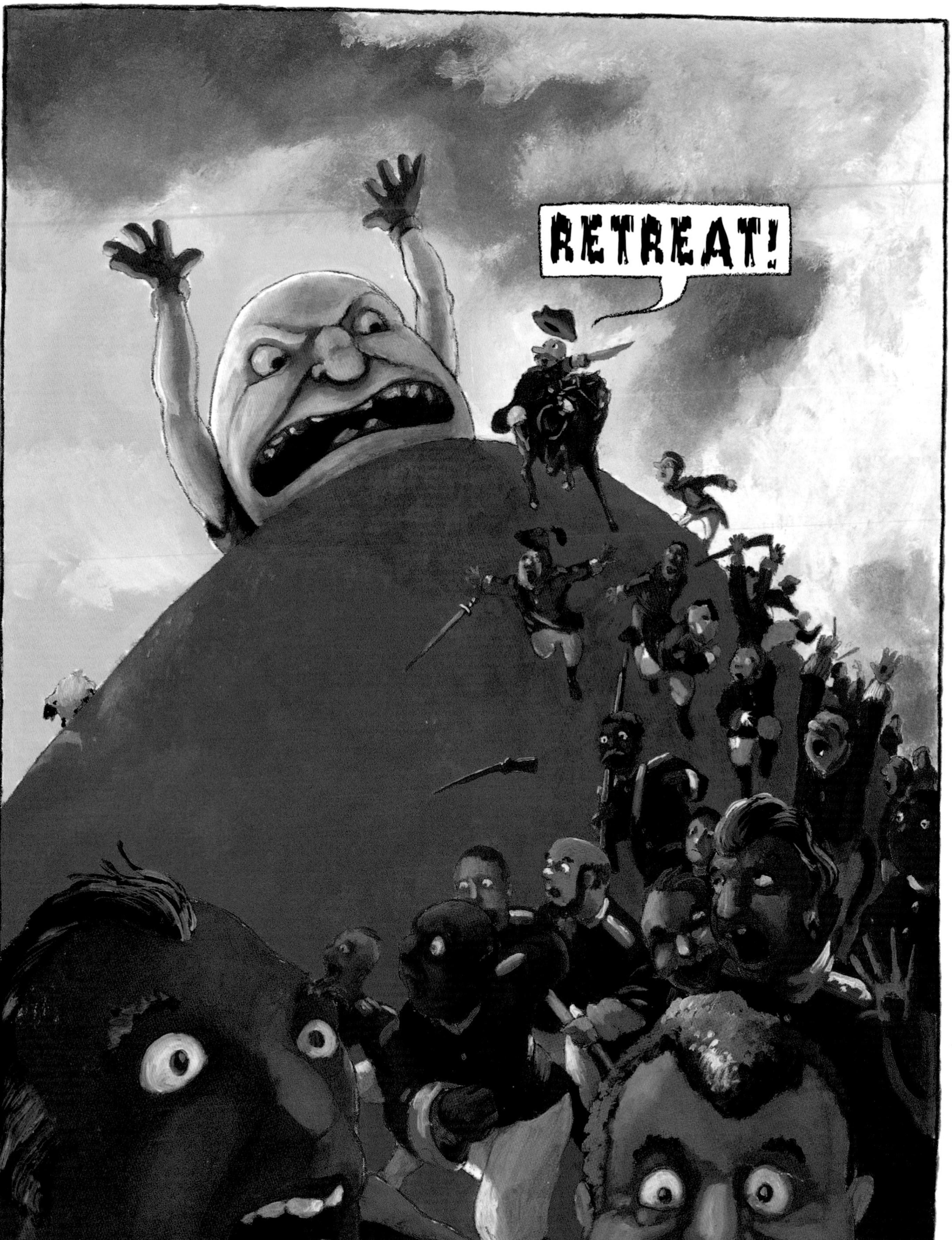
RETREAT!

"No good, Sire," said Jack. "He marched them all straight up the hill and he marched them down again."

"I should have known," said the king.

"I could try the Old Woman That Lives in the Shoe," said Jack.

"Naw, she's got so many children,
she won't know what to do," said the king.

"Sire?" yelled Jack, "Come quick! Humpty's crashing through the town!"

Humpty Dumpty was on a rampage.
He found Jack Horner sitting in the corner.
He stole his plum, Christmas pie and all.

He sat on Little Miss Muffet's tuffet
and ate all her curds and whey.
He shook the whole town.
Things were looking bad.

"I've got it," said Old King Cole.
"You know Peter . . . Peter Pumpkin Eater?"

"Oh sure. I heard his wife got out of the pumpkin shell. I believe she's doing very well," said Jack.

"Yes, yes, yes. Go and tell Peter to roll that pumpkin downtown.
I want him to stuff Humpty in it."

"I've got it!" barked Old King Cole. "Do you know the Muffin Man?"

"The Muffin Man?" asked Jack.

"The Muffin Man! Do you know the Muffin Man?" asked the king.

"Oh sure," said Jack, "he lives on Drurey Lane."

"Well, go to him and tell him to lay a path of muffins down Main Street.
Tell him to make a left onto Wall Street.
We'll drive Humpty Dumpty right up the wall," said the king.

Roses are red,
violets are blue.
Pumpkins
are orange,
and the town is too.

Wrecking a town is hard work. Humpty was really hungry.
He followed the muffin trail just as Old King Cole had hoped.
The enraged eggman climbed right up the wall and sat there eating a huge pile of muffins.

"Now we have to find a way to push him off. That'll knock some sense into him," said the king.

"Sire, Sire! Dr. Foster, on his way to Gloucester, reports that Mother Goose is on her way back home," said Jack.

"Thank goodness," said Old King Cole. "Now I can get back to being merry."

Mother Goose flew in the window.

"The town's a mess. What's going on here?

I can't even go away for the weekend without this place going to pieces."
Old King Cole filled Mother Goose in about Humpty Dumpty's rampage.

"Get me all the king's horses and all the king's men," yelled Mother Goose.
"Send them all to the wall!"

"Yes Ma'am!" said Jack.

Meanwhile,

Humpty was almost finished with his muffins.
He was extremely full.
He was getting very sleepy.
His eyes were beginning to close.
He started to slip off the wall.

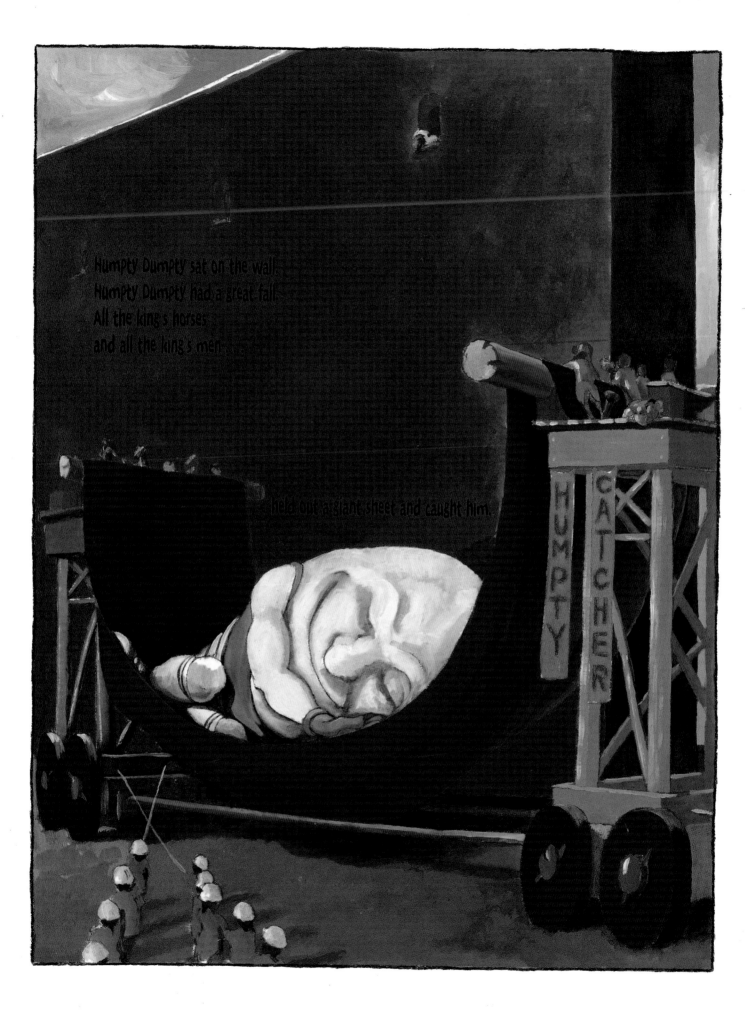

Humpty Dumpty sat on the wall.
Humpty Dumpty had a great fall.
All the king's horses
and all the king's men . . .

held out a giant sheet and caught him.

"What are you going to do with him now?" asked Jack.

"Get me Gregory Griggs."

"Gregory Griggs?
Had twenty-seven different wigs?
He wore them up, he wore them down
to please the people of the town?" asked Jack.

"Yes, yes, yes. Now tell him to bring all his wigs," said Mother Goose.

Mother Goose stitched all the wigs together
and gently lowered the hair onto Humpty's head.

When Humpty
woke up,
he had a fine
head of hair.

With his egg-citing new look and attitude, Humpty Dumpty became a big star.
He does two shows a day and when he falls, the crowd goes wild.

SLEEP DISORDERS

Dr. Little Boy Blue

Good Garden

MARY

CONTRARY PUB

My Life with Dog

Old Woman

TOM, TOM...
THE
PIPER'S
SON

SAGA PUB

Make Pies CHEAP!

VOL.1

SIMPLE SIMON
VIDEO